W9-APX-777

IN THE HAUNTED HOUSE

BY EVE BUNTING

Illustrated by
SUSAN MEDDAUGH

Clarion Books - New York

Pencil and watercolor were used to
create the full-color art in this book.
The text type is 16 pt. ITC Zapf International Light.

Clarion Books
a Houghton Mifflin Company imprint
215 Park Avenue South, New York, NY 10003
Text copyright © 1990 by Eve Bunting
Illustrations copyright © 1990 by Susan Meddaugh
Printed in the USA

Library of Congress Cataloging-in-Publication Data
Bunting, Eve, 1928-
In the haunted house / by Eve Bunting ; illustrated by Susan
Meddaugh.
p.   cm.
Summary: A little girl and her father tour a dark, mysterious
house, eventually revealed to be a "Halloween House."
PA ISBN 0-395-69942-8   ISBN 0-395-51589-0
[1. Haunted houses—Fiction.   2. Fathers and daughters—Fiction.
3. Halloween—Fiction.]   I. Meddaugh, Susan, ill.   II. Title.
PZ7.B91527In   1990
[E]—dc20   89-77663
                                                   CIP
                                                   AC

WOZ 10 9 8

For the twins, Tory and Erin, with love
—E.B.

To John and Justin
—S.M.

This is the house where the scary ones hide.
Open the door and step softly inside.

An organ is playing a funeral air.
It's playing and playing, but nobody's there.

Ghosts swim in the hallway, three witches appear.

Bats hang by their feet from the cracked chandelier.

"Give me your hand, you're as brave as can be!
I know you're not frightened, but stay close to me."

At the top of the stairs, where the long cobwebs drift,
Is a box with a lid that says DO NOT LIFT.

The mirror that hangs on the dark, paneled wall
Shows faces that don't look like faces at all.

A mummy's in bed and it's dead as can be,
So why does its dead eye keep winking at me?

And who's in the closet, dark as a tomb,
Rattling his bones in the gloom-gloomy-gloom?

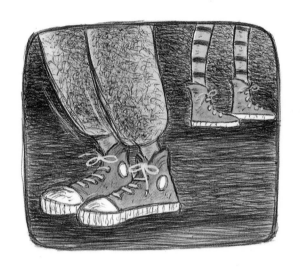

"*I know you're not frightened, but still…we could go.*
No one would notice. 'No,' you say? 'No'?"

The roof space is creeping and crawling with things,

Things that have horns and raggedy wings.

There's a coffin-shaped tub, claw-footed and deep,
And in it's a vampire who smiles in his sleep.

At the basin a werewolf is washing his snout,
Sucking in water and spouting it out.

"Is someone behind us? I don't want to look!
It might be a zombie! It might be a spook!"

We're back where we started, the bats are still there.
The organ's still playing a funeral air.

It's time to go home, to step softly outside.
Out of the house where the scary things hide,

Into the day that's asparkle with sun.

Halloween Houses are so much fun!